I0699989

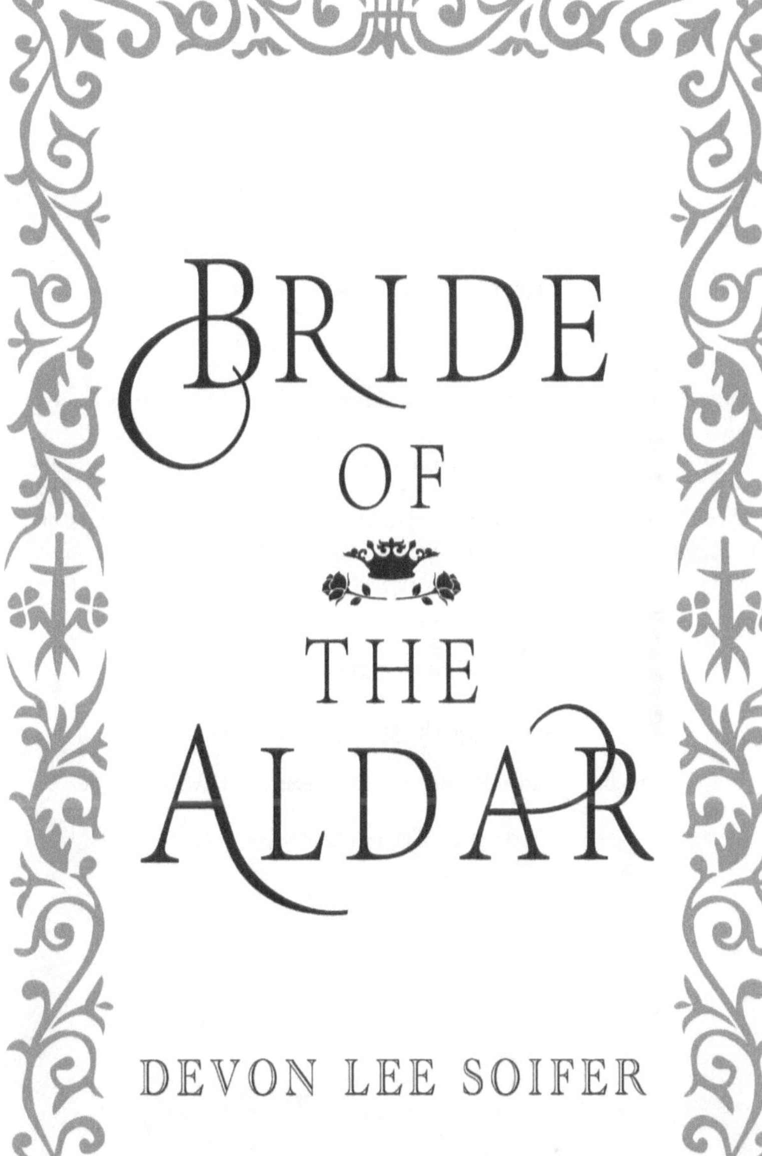

BRIDE OF THE ALDAR

DEVON LEE SOIFER

ISBN 979-8-9864235-2-4

Cover & Book Design: Devon Lee Soifer

Cover Photos: Christian Holzinger via Shutterstock / Devon Lee Soifer

Map Design: Devon Lee Soifer

To Eric and Claire
For supporting me and cheering me on

Content Warning

This story includes references to
or depictions of the following:

Abortion
Bigotry
Corporal punishment
Parosmia
Self-harm
Sexual intercourse
Sexual assault

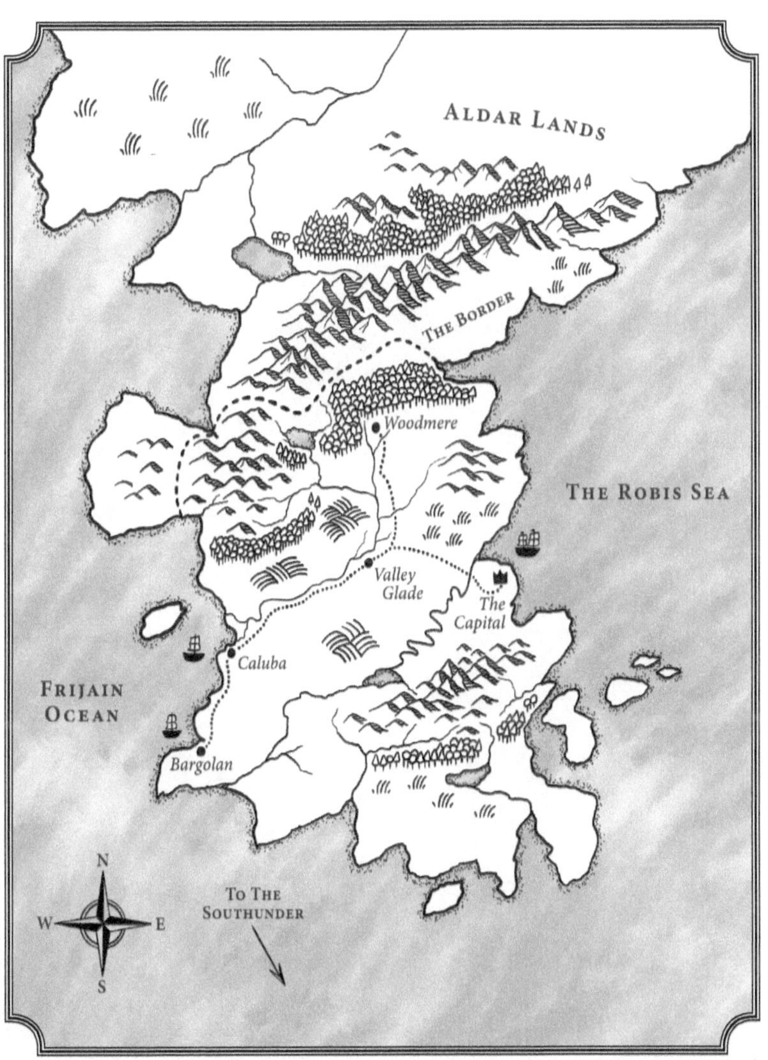

ALDAR LANDS
THE BORDER
Woodmere
THE ROBIS SEA
Valley Glade
The Capital
FRIJAIN OCEAN
Caluba
Bargolan
N
W
E
S
TO THE SOUTHUNDER

BRIDE OF THE ALDAR

Many of the things the elders told us weren't true. Perhaps they were once true, but no longer, at least as far as my friend Lus and I had been able to discern.

The fortress on the mount, for example, was not cursed, nor was it full of traps. We should not have known this, as we were forbidden from going there. We explored the ruins several times, though Lus took some convincing at first. We went after Ritual, when we could tell our parents we were gathering wildflowers or mushrooms, depending on the time of year. Other than its age and its imposing height overlooking Valley Glade, there was nothing remarkable about the old castle, nothing sinister. We kept going back because it was a secret that belonged just to us. After Initiation, nothing would be our own. Even our souls would belong to our husbands.

I had never been afraid of things that didn't appear

dangerous at first. This earned me a few scrapes and scars as a little girl, to my mother's continued exasperation. Fine, unmarked skin is highly prized among the Initiated. When I was old enough to start working in the tavern, my lack of fear made me well suited for staying calm around our clientele. For generations, my family had run the only establishment in the village that served the Aldar.

Aldar visitors were rare so far from the border. Most of our patrons were fellow humans, a mix of thrifty travelers, curious oddballs, and those who couldn't afford anything better. The only wealthy guests we ever saw were the Aldar, or the few merchants who did business with them. I think that's why my great-grandfather decided to keep serving the Aldar, even though he'd fought against them in the last war. The Aldar always had gold, sometimes gems. We offered them some semblance of dignity in a place where they were otherwise unwelcome. They came to our tavern to meet with their associates in peace.

I was not to look at them when they came in. No human female was allowed to look at or speak to an Aldar. This was supposed to remind them of our chastity and discourage them from bewitching us. My father, or the cook Egold, typically greeted them and brought them to the trio of booths at the back—tables and benches built tall to accommodate

Aldar stature—or up to the best rooms on the top floor. If neither man was available, I could make an exception and serve them, though I couldn't make eye contact. I was eighteen before I ever broke this rule, and I blame Lus. Truthfully, I could blame Lus for the entire unraveling of my life from that moment onward. I could blame her, but I could also thank her.

I was wiping the tables by the dusty front window when I heard hissing from behind the bar. Egold had gone around back with my father to receive the ale shipment, so I had the tavern to myself except for a handful of drowsy-looking patrons clustered at tables by the hearth.

"Bel," the hiss said. "Bel!"

I ignored it for one more moment, then tossed the rag I'd been using over the bar top. A damp thwack was followed by a whine of disgust.

"You don't need to hide," I said. "No demons in today."

That's another lie the elders tell, that the Aldar are demons. If they are, then demons are tall and beautiful, which is not what they tell us at Ritual.

Lus popped up from behind the bar, clamping her maiden's cap back down on her head. She threw the rag at me. "Ugh, it smells of piss."

"It smells of dried ale, nothing else." I returned to wiping tables and Lus followed me. "I'm working until sunset. What has you in here hissing at me instead of helping your own parents?"

"Lady Mordred has published the Order of Initiation. I got an early peek at it!" Lus's parents were printers who often completed orders for both the Sacred House and the Council. Lady Mordred was the leader of the Consort of Families, the group of holy women and councilors' wives who approved matches between the village's young people every year. She had the ultimate say over the order in which the eligible girls were brought through the Ceremony of Initiation, which declared them part of the congregation and therefore eligible to marry. It was widely acknowledged that the girls who went first were considered the most accomplished, beautiful, and desirable.

"Oh really?" I did my best to match Lus's enthusiasm. She'd been looking forward to this ever since the first hints of womanhood took hold of her body. It was easy to anticipate the day if one's qualities were the type generally considered the most charming. Lus was slender and petite, though not so petite as to hint at malnutrition. Her lips and cheeks were so rosy the schoolmaster had once accused her of wearing rouge and made her wipe her face vigorously with vinegar to prove that she wasn't. Being raised in a house full of books and pamphlets had given her ample opportunity to memorize and compose poetry. And her biggest charm of all was a wealthy and influential father.

"Shall I guess where you placed?" I asked, tapping my temple in mock contemplation. "Let's see. Isabet will be first, of course. No one will be surprised."

Lus rolled her eyes and nodded. "Yes, but—"

"Nadey is either second or third, depending how Lady Mordred feels about Ulra's blemishes." I ignored Lus prancing around me anxiously as I made damp spirals on the pockmarked table.

"Bel—"

"And she wouldn't dare put a shepherd's daughter like Yana above you…so that makes you fourth!" I smacked the table triumphantly with the rag.

"Yes, but Bel, that's not the best of it!" Lus took hold of my wrists, clutching them against her chest. "You're sixth!"

I jerked away from her grip. I had never expected to break the top ten. I might not have broken the top twenty had there been more than that many girls to choose from in our year. "That's not funny, Lus."

"I'm not making fun. I saw it with my own eyes." If those very same eyes had not been as round as marbles with earnestness, I might not have believed her. Lus was a terrible liar, which was why she was so afraid of breaking the rules.

Before I had a chance to respond, the front door of the tavern swung open behind me.

Not a soul would believe me if I told them, but I thought he was a human at first glance. With all the boys our age away at the King's Academies, perhaps I'd just forgotten what young human men looked like. Truly, it was his hair that fooled me. Most Aldar have pale hair from white to dark blond, straight as ironed silk. This one had a cascade of dark red that curled at the ends. Not what humans call red, like the dusty copper brown of my own hair. I mean red like berry-flavored tea or autumn leaves before they fall to the earth.

The color was enough to confuse me, so when he first stepped in the door, I turned to him without thinking and said, "Good morrow, brother." Only when I lifted my head from my bow did I realize my mistake. He stared down at me, and it was as if the fire had leapt from the hearth and burned up all the air in the room. "I mean…sir."

Only men addressed an Aldar as "sir" or "madam." I don't know why I said it, except that I felt a powerful need to respond to those moss green eyes in some way.

"Bel!" Lus hissed. I heard her shoes scuffing across the floor as she hastily retreated behind the bar again, leaving me to my fate. Her horrified exclamation released me from my shock, and I lowered my head, spreading my hands, palms up, in a gesture of subservient greeting. The other patrons' conversations had fallen silent. I started counting witnesses to my crime as I waited for the Aldar man to speak. At my eye level, the tips of his crimson hair curled against the brushed gray suede of his cloak.

"I wish for a meal and a chamber for the night," he said at last. His voice was like the lowest string on a Cardolan harp, deep and precise. I nodded and he followed me to a booth at the back. "A refreshment if you please," he said, shifting his cloak from his broad shoulders and handing it to me. I couldn't help admiring the silver brocade doublet he wore beneath, patterned with curling fern fronds and clusters of acorns. It reminded me of the wooded glen that Lus and I hiked through to get up to the fortress without being seen from the village. The Aldar were originally forest folk, and it showed in their crafts. I hung his cloak and went to fetch an ale. Predictably, Lus had snuck out the back door. I hoped she'd run to fetch my father. Then again, I hoped she hadn't.

When I returned with the drink, the Aldar had extended a leg from under the table and was examining his boot with a frown. One of its silver buckles had torn free from its strap, leaving the top of the boot partially open. He looked up at me abruptly.

"Are there any decent cobblers in this village?"

I nodded and curtsied.

"Where might I find him?"

I bit my lip and turned my face away. First off, Valley Glade's best cobbler was a widow, not a man. Her shop was in an alley down toward the river, not easily seen from the main road unless you knew where to look. Secondly, he should have known better than to ask anything but a yes or no question of a human girl. The other patrons were sneaking frequent glances toward his table. If anyone told my father I had talked to an Aldar, he'd be obligated to punish me. If he didn't, the Council would punish him, and likely my mother too.

The Aldar sighed and put his cup down on the table. "I know your menfolk would have me think that you are mute. You have already shown me that is not true. I hope you would not be so inhospitable as to make me wait for your master's return to answer such a simple question."

Caught between nodding, *Yes, our menfolk would have you think I'm mute,* and, *No, I don't mean to be inhospitable,* the best I could do was stare at the back of the booth and widen my eyes, hoping it conveyed my frustration at his breach of etiquette.

"Very well. Turn toward the wall as you walk away and say it quietly." His tone was bored yet commanding, as if he were used to getting his way. I bristled at being ordered about by a stranger, but for some reason, I did as he said.

"It's not simple," I whispered. "I'll have to write it down."

The Aldar knew enough not to nod or acknowledge my statement in any way. I scurried back to the bar like the meek human girl I should have been. I tore a corner off an old broadsheet and scribbled "Widow Cork - Cobbler" on it. Below that, I drew a rough map of the town with the main street and the river, a line between them indicating the alley. Egold walked in as I folded the note. I grabbed the cook's elbow.

"Egold, there's an Aldar," I said.

"Oh!" Egold squinted his watery eyes at the back booth. Though he was only a few years older than me, he could barely see, which accounted for his being out of the Service already. "Peculiar looking one, isn't he?"

Almost as if he'd heard the comment, the Aldar swept his dark hair back from his forehead. I saw this out of the corner of my eye. I'd never felt the urge to stare at an Aldar before, yet something about this simple gesture made my head twitch his direction of its own accord. I closed my fist around the note in my palm.

"He wants a meal," I said.

"Alright, alright," Egold sighed. "There are two more crates to bring to the cellar and your father went to the butcher."

"Just heat something up. I'll bring it to him."

A short while later, I brought a steaming plate of stewed vegetables and grilled fish to the Aldar. As I set the food before him, I let the corner of the note peek out from under the plate's rim. He saw it immediately and covered it with a long-fingered hand.

As I withdrew, he said, "Thank you, sister." I nearly tripped over my own feet in surprise. He'd addressed me as if he were a fellow human, as I had mistakenly done when he first walked in. My head still bowed demurely, I glanced at him to see a smile curling at the corner of his mouth. I had never seen an Aldar smile before.

I spent the rest of the night after my shift waiting for my father to burst into our private apartments above the tavern with his flogging whip in hand. My father had never relished such punishment, only resorting to it when my behavior made it unavoidable. It had been years since he'd had to do it. My mother had started to worry that my future husband would spot the scars left by the welts and question my meager dowry. There was a reason whipping was the proscribed punishment for girls—obedience was the highest virtue. A disobedient woman would hold the marks of her transgressions on her flesh forever. Rather than let my parents continue to argue over my skin, I simply got better at not getting caught when I broke the rules.

Somehow, none of the patrons told my father about my slip-up with the Aldar. I could only conclude that they came from regions where the separation of the peoples was not so strictly followed as in Valley Glade.

I didn't see Lus again until a day and half later, when we met up after Ritual as usual. She hugged me as if I'd come back from the dead.

"Blood of saints! What were you thinking?"

"I don't know," I said. "I wasn't." Something about the red-haired Aldar made all cautious thoughts vanish from my mind. I'd almost gotten caught staring at him twice more, as I watched my father bow and scrape before him and the human merchants who came to meet with him. His stay had been mercifully brief. He'd departed that morning, and my mind had turned back to what had distracted me in the first place. The Order of Initiation had been posted at the Council Hall, and I had now seen for myself that Lus was right. My name was sixth on the list.

"Lady Mordred must have been impressed with your

recitations," Lus ventured as we climbed through the glen with our gathering baskets hanging from our elbows. I'd convinced her I needed the fresh air up at the fortress to clear my head.

I scoffed. "We both know that can't be true." While I hadn't lost my place during my recitation before the Consort of Families, I had stumbled over half a dozen words, hardly demonstrating the eloquence expected when entertaining one's husband.

Lus brought up a few more of my feeble accomplishments and I steadily knocked them down one after the other. By the time we reached the fortress, she'd run out. In silence, we wended our way through the half-tumbled walls and grass-covered mounds of fallen masonry. We settled side-by-side on a ledge that had once been the sill of a tall arched window. It faced north, away from the village. Rolling fields spread out before us, dotted with sheep. Beyond, thickets gave way to forests, which climbed up to mist-swathed mountains in the distance. Looking north made me think of the border, reminding me of the red-haired Aldar. I shook his face—green eyes, thick lashes—from my mind.

"I have a suspicion as to why I was so high on the list," I said.

"Really?" Lus said far too brightly. I knew she hoped I would finally give myself a compliment.

"My mother," I said.

Both my parents were overjoyed at my unexpected achievement. But as they'd plied me with honeyed cakes and berry tea, I'd noticed that neither of them seemed very surprised. A few days later, as I helped sweep out the small apothecary shop my mother kept beside the tavern, I found the nerve to ask her about it.

"What did you do to raise my prospects?" I asked.

"I've told you a thousand times, Bel'eva, you must not be so direct with your questions. It smacks of insolence."

I held back a sigh. "May I enquire if I owe it to your credit that I have somehow achieved beyond the position I deserve?"

"Deserve! Oh, Bel'eva." My mother shook her head and caressed my shoulder. "Of course you deserve this. All of us do."

"All of us?"

"You, me, and your father." She raised her chin in her imperious way. "The last of the Hombord clan."

"We aren't the last. What of cousin Alfez?"

"The last with any honor, then."

"How did you do it?"

My mother clapped her hands then folded them together.

"Your father was offered the position of a junior councilor. He believes he should be on the High Council, if anywhere. No one in his clan has ever taken a lesser seat. I reminded him that many juniors are moved up when the high councilors…depart. Still, he would not see my way. I suggested to a few councilors' wives that if they could raise your standing, your father would relent and take the lower position, confident that his family remained in high esteem. So it was arranged."

I couldn't help marveling at her scheming, even though the revelation hurt. Until that moment, I had held out hope that the Consort of Families had seen something in me that I did not see in myself, and had placed me sixth of their own accord.

My mother must have taken my expression as derision, which wasn't far off. "When you are my age, you will have a greater respect for the value of having a lineage. Especially if the saints only bless you with one child." She took the broom from me and told me to dust the shelves behind the counter while she re-swept the floor. I half listened to her matron's gossip as we worked, until she said, "We're fortunate that we had an Aldar guest recently. We'll be able to afford a finer dress for you for the Fete of Choosing. I told your father you'll need something quite grand to fit your ranking."

I had never given much thought to my Choosing dress, assuming that I would be in the background, hardly scrutinized. I was not prepared for the many rounds of fittings that ensued, with me standing stalk still on a wood block while my mother and the seamstress cooed and quibbled over the design. The process humiliated me, as did Lus's questions about it later. Having been evaded on the topic of wardrobe, she turned to boys.

"How do you think they will have changed?" she mused as I helped her hang freshly printed papers to dry in her parents' shop. "Do you think many of them will be tall?"

Nearly three years had passed since we'd last seen the boys from our Initiation year. We'd all gone to the small school together. Once they went to the King's Academies, the only news of them came from letters to their families, sparse details of which made the rounds of the village as gossip. Boys with whom one had shared even the slightest affection grew into heroic lovers by dint of absence. While officially the debut of maidens, the Fete of Choosing also brought the boys back to the village as men for the first time.

"Cadef might be tall," I said. "Both his brothers are. And his sister."

"That's true. Poor Amilla."

I tried not to grumble, remembering my mother and the

seamstress arguing about how the dress might make my own height appear elegant, rather than lanky.

"At least we may be thankful the Mordreds are a year behind us," Lus said, face twisted as if she'd had a close whiff of the ink pots. "I can hardly believe such scoundrels are now earning special commendations." Lady Mordred's nephews, cousins named Nafene and Gabol, were the nemeses of any girl they considered neither as compliant nor beautiful as they liked. They teased Lus for her large eyes and sloped shoulders, and me for my hair, though in truth I think they hated me because I stared right back at them, neither crying nor yelling in response to their groping or insults. I highly doubted time away at a military school had humbled them.

"Yes," I said. "Thank the saints for that."

I grew nervous as the Fete approached. I ought to have been put over the edge when the red-haired Aldar reappeared at our tavern, but he was a welcome distraction. I didn't talk to him again, and only my father served him. I spent as much time in the tavern as possible, making excuses to trade tasks with Egold for a chance to sneak glances at the Aldar. Half the time, I caught him staring back at me. Had he been a human patron, I would have marched over and made him awkward with my overattentiveness. Since I could do no such thing, I just kept looking. He wore the same cloak as before, but with a pale green and gold doublet and breeches beneath. I noticed that both his boots were securely buckled.

My parents made me stop working two days before the Fete, to preserve the condition of my hands and complexion. The night before, my mother bathed me herself, as she hadn't done since I was young, going so far as to scent my hair with rose water. The strong appetite she'd often chastised me for was entirely absent the next morning. Confined to our apartments, I watched through the window as the Aldar strode out into the tavern yard to meet a carriage. Another Aldar stepped out of it. He was much more the type one would expect: pale, straw-like hair, thin-limbed with a slightly pinched face. My Aldar did almost look human by comparison, I decided, with his dark hair, broad jaw, and square-tipped nose. The two Aldar touched their hands to their chests and bowed to each other, then departed together in the carriage.

When the time came, it felt like someone else's hair was being braided and pinned high. Someone else's hands were rubbed with fragranced oil. The mirror was a portrait of a stranger. I had never seen a more magnificent dress. A skirt of layered chiffon cascaded from my hips and pooled behind me in a train. The sleeves were belled and so long that they covered all but my fingertips, the hem of their oblong cuffs tickling the floor. The bodice was brilliant silver brocade, in a pattern like wind-whipped clouds, and came to a point a few inches below my stomach. White pearls strung on knotted silver cord shimmered above the full curve of my breasts. Above it all were the wary dark eyes of a creature of prey.

My mother walked behind us, carrying my train, as I entered the Fete on my father's elbow. The walls of the council hall had been draped in cloth, and hundreds of fresh candles burned in candelabras and sconces, making the tall room as bright as afternoon. Where the chief councilor's podium usually stood, the matrons and priestesses of the Consort of Families were hurriedly arranging maidens into a long, curved line.

Lus murmured, "No," when she saw me, her mouth hanging open after the vowel expired on her lips. Matron Lydia quickly shushed her, but she stared and stared at me after I took my place in line. Yana, standing between us, gave me one long look, then kept her face resolutely forward, despite Lus staring past her. I tried to smile at my friend and gave a subtle shrug. Lus mouthed, "Wow," then smoothed her hands over her own skirts. I recognized parts of her mother's bridal dress, which we had secretly drawn from its chest several times as girls. The fabric had been dyed green to complement Lus's coiffe of dark curls.

A brisk but passionless tapping on the Council drum drew the chamber to silence. Parents, siblings, and Council members gathered toward the walls, making a corridor between them. The drum started up again, and a sibilant tremor went through the maidens as the boys appeared through the door at the opposite end of the hall.

Not boys—men—marching toward us in rows. They were all taller than they had been. Many were broader too. I had trouble recognizing a few of them beneath the whiskers that had sprouted on their chins and cheeks. They were a formidable presence, in their matching blue academy coats with the brown upturned collars and cuffs, ornate saber scabbards clipped to sashes at their hips. With precision, they spread themselves out in a line to match our own, but with a gap at the center to allow for an aisle.

"What in heaven?" I heard Lus whisper. I followed her gaze. On the right flank, the Mordred cousins stood side-by-side, smugly surveying the arrayed maidens. Their aunt swept into the open floor between the lines, her dour gown and mien brightened only by the large ceremonial amulet on a thick chain around her neck.

"Welcome, brothers and sisters, to the Fete of Choosing." She had a singer's voice, and it carried in the large space, hushing the speculative twittering of the crowd. "By this tradition we honor the holy precepts and ensure their continuation through the generations. We are joyful for the return of our sons, who by honor and diligence have become soldiers in his Majesty's Army. And we are grateful to the fathers who have brought their girl children to us, so they may become brides."

Signaled by a swish of Lady Mordred's hand, all of us maidens took a half step forward and bowed, the sound of so much shifting fabric like a gust of wind. My heart pounded as we straightened, because I was suddenly me again. I was the one in the absurdly beautiful dress with impractically long sleeves. I was the one bowing before a group of boys, who, last we met, were not entertained by poetry or music or any of the other charms we girls had been taught, but by competing to see who could get slapped the hardest without falling over. The fathers who had led us up to the stage on which we stood, they had been those boys once too. They still were, for what was my father's aspiration for a seat on the Council but a quest for a meaningless accomplishment that lifted him ever so slightly above his peers?

I glanced along the line of maidens. Some looked how I felt, as if they were standing outside on a harsh winter day without a cloak. Others were placid, as if watching a troupe of actors performing a play in which they had no part. A rare few stood tall with pride, smiling back at the boys who eyed us like dogs eager for the hunt.

As the panic rose within me, Lady Mordred called the first boy forward. His name was Luca, wide-faced with floppy brown hair and a tendency to laugh even if a joke outwitted him. He came to the center of the floor and kneeled. As if he were reading from a page, he said, "Luca Nertecamo Jos chooses the daughter of house Amrosea."

Far to my left, Nitaz Amrosea the cooper's daughter, stepped forward and inclined her head. Luca rose and led her to a row of chairs set along the back of the room. Before they had left, the next boy was kneeling.

"Eget Randecamo Floriz chooses the daughter of house Bluma."

The air became thick in my lungs as I watched Lus step forward, the stone floor catching briefly on the hem of her dress. Eget, the boy with eyes so pale we used to call him the Ghost, came forward and clasped my friend's hand. I wanted her to look back at me. I wanted to make a sound. I had not expected her to be chosen so early. There was no rule that said we had to be chosen in the order we were presented. The Order of Initiation was published before the Fete as a formality, a guide or families who had not yet submitted their betrothal claim to the Council, but its only official purpose was to say what order the maidens would approach the apse at our Sacred Initiation a few months from now.

"Cadef Shegarcamo Palot chooses the daughter of house Mkeddy." Ulra Mkeddy bowed and joined her betrothed.

"Waldon Ertlecamo Nahinda chooses the daughter of house Pelair." Yana Pelair bowed and joined her betrothed.

And so it went, the crowd clapping politely after each pairing, their families' heads turning to watch them. Half a dozen more couples descended the aisle to the waiting chairs. My mind began to dissociate from my body again, drifting to some place where my true self was still intact. Then I heard, "Nafene Harodcamo Mordred"—I balled my fists inside my sleeves—"chooses the daughter of house Cyleao."

Gabol Mordred let out a whoop as his cousin rose and took the hand of Isabet Cyleao, daughter of the richest man in town, besides his own grandfather. Isabet beamed, gliding forward in her bead-encrusted marigold yellow dress.

"Gabol Jakarcamo Mordred chooses the daughter of house Hombord."

The whine in my ears from my tightly clenched jaw was so loud that I was unsure if I had heard correctly, but Gabol stared right up at me, purplish lips curved. I stepped forward and bowed my head. Distantly, I had heard an intake of breath and somehow knew it was my mother's. I raised my chin. The sheath of Gabol's sword clacked noisily against the buckle of his boot when he stopped in front of me. He took my hand before I even lifted it from my side. As we descended the aisle, he walked faster than I could go in my dress. I pulled back against his hand. He glanced at me and pulled it forward again. Forced to match his pace, my slippers nipped the hem of my skirt, threatening to trip me with every step. By the time we reached the chairs, my legs were wobbly as a new calf's.

I took my seat with some relief, trying to catch Lus's eye down the row. Then I noticed that Gabol had not released my hand. Through the gauzy fabric of my sleeve, his grip was heavy and damp.

"Surprised to see me?" he asked. When I didn't immediately respond, he repeated. "Hey, Bel, you surprised to see me?"

I managed a nod.

"Special commendation. Both me and Naf. Saved the Admiral's holy crest from a fire. His herald too, the idiot."

I stared at him blankly. What did the Admiral's holy standard and its bearer have to do with our betrothal?

Gabol sputtered his exasperation. "We were rewarded

for doing a divine service. Promoted early."

"Oh," I said. "I see."

"Didn't you hear of it? I wrote my mother. She said people have not stopped talking to her about me." Both he and his cousin, and their aunt for that matter, had nearly lashless eyes, their rims always slightly pink, as if the hairs had recently been plucked. My own eyes watered when I met his.

"Yes, I think I did," I said. I shifted my hand. Gabol only took it as an invitation to hold tighter. He kept holding it until he was forced to switch to my other hand during our traditional first dance. I didn't dare wipe the remnants of his gummy sweat on my dress. I gripped the shoulder of his uniform instead. The wool was rougher than I expected, rougher than anything that should come up against bare skin.

Gabol's hand was low on my back as he dragged me through the steps and turns. I knew the dance, but again he was too fast. When I couldn't keep up, he pulled me against him so tightly that my feet left the floor. I was at his mercy until he finished the steps and my toes found the floor again. During one spin, he sniffed my hair.

"You make my mouth water," he said. "But they should have put a veil on you, like some of the others." We spun again, his thick arm taking my weight like it was nothing.

"Too many men have seen your hair already. Don't know why your mother lets you out of the house so often without your maiden cap."

"It's on purpose," I said past my compressed ribs. "She puts lemon in my hair so the sun will turn it yellow."

Gabol gave a growling chuckle. "Thank the saints brown overpowers ginger in the blood. You won't give me any ginger-headed children. So, no bleaching them with juice. Save the lemons for my tea and whisky."

I strained to hear the harp amidst the other instruments that were playing, waiting for a low note that would remind me of a different person, a different voice. The music was ending, but somehow, I was still spinning. Spinning.

I spun through the rest of the Fete, through the carriage ride home, through my mother praising me as she removed the dress and folded it away. I was still spinning at Ritual a day later. I was so turned around that I went right home afterward, and Lus had to come find me. I sat on the rug before the fire in our apartments. I heard her greet my mother and climb the stairs. She approached me like someone might approach the bedside of the gravely ill.

"Why?" I asked her. "Why did he pick me? We're not wealthy. I'm not charming or accomplished or beautiful."

Lus kneeled beside me. "You're not poor. And you're not

charmless or useless or ugly."

"He thinks my hair is ugly. That I'm immodest for not wearing my cap—as if he's one to preach such things."

"Bel, I'm so sorry." Sorry for my plight, and sorry she had merely gotten Eget the Ghost. His only objectionable trait was that he was too plain to have anything objectionable about him.

"Gabol pushed me down and kissed me once when we were younger," I said. "It was like kissing the slime on rotting chicken meat."

Lus licked her lips through a grimace. We had both kissed boys before, traipsing along the edge of sin by inviting them to touch us, put their hands beneath our skirts or down the front of our loosened bodices. We touched them back. All of us were reckless the year before the boys left for the Academies, but Gabol was relentless. He did not wait for an invitation. He never would.

"The rest of my life," I muttered. "The rest of my life. I don't know how I will survive."

Lus said nothing. All we could do was stare into the fireplace, at the soot-stained brick holding the burning within.

I was never more observant of any holy precept than the one that forbade a newly betrothed girl from interacting with her intended before her Initiation. This precept was not always part of the Holy Will, as the elders say it was. The rule was added less than a century ago to stem the tide of misbegotten children who arrived in the unsteady years after the last war. Even now, hardly every couple kept chaste, and it was clear by how Gabol stared at me at Ritual that he did not wish to. But we were the most talked about betrothal in the village, and thus closely watched. He would not get close to me if I did not let him, and I was fiercely determined to do the opposite.

I spent as many hours working in the tavern as my parents would let me. They had become oddly indulgent after the betrothal, as if my unexpectedly prestigious match had absolved me of previous unruliness. Or they simply saw their job of raising me as finished. I would marry well, that was all that mattered.

Amidst serving and clearing tables, collecting payment from overnight guests, and pouring drinks, I found my eyes jumped to the door every time an unusually tall silhouette appeared in its frame. Weeks passed before an Aldar came in. I stood stiffly before a polished wall sconce, pretending to steady the candle as I watched the door behind me in the reflection. But the Aldar was blond. In the blurry image, I recognized him as the one who had come with the carriage before. His presence was a tease.

I abandoned the sconce, turning back to my basket of tallow candles. The blond Aldar remained at the entry. As Egold rushed to greet him, another figure stepped in. I forced my eyes away from the unmistakable shade of red. I kept to my task as placidly as I could, replacing even the barely burned candles with new ones, though I pointedly skipped the ones above the Aldar booths. I knew the red-haired Aldar was watching me as I went about the tavern. I could feel it. Even if he never looked at me once, he was watching me.

Once again, my father served the Aldar while merchants came and went from their booth. The blond Aldar did most of the talking. The red-haired Aldar only seemed to speak when prompted, supplying information that the other needed for his negotiations. When evening fell and the crowd that came for business was replaced by the crowd that came for drink, I went to tidy the guestrooms. I had overheard enough to know the Aldar were both staying the night. I prepared two chambers with special attention and care, not knowing which of them would choose which room.

When I was done, I went down the narrow stairs to help with supper service, only to find the way blocked by someone coming up. It was the red-haired Aldar.

I lowered my face and curtsied. From below my brows, I saw him bow back.

"Hello," he said. "It's a pleasure to see you again."

I lifted my chin and met his eyes. He smiled slightly. So did I.

"You must have dazzled them in that silver gown," the Aldar said. I let my mouth fall open in surprise. He cocked his head. "We're alone. No one can hear you but me."

"You were there?" I whispered.

"They would have sooner stabbed me than let me through the doors. I merely assumed that the bolts of Aldar silk your father bought from me were not for his shirts and I don't see any new drapes in this old place."

I thought of how the silver fabric had moved with me, slipping along my skin like a caress every time I lifted my arms, swirling about my ankles as I walked. How the bodice had held me yet moved with me.

"Even in your people's simple styles, no doubt it was a garment befitting an Aldar princess," he said. "Had I been there, perhaps I would have mistaken you for one."

My stomach jolted as if I'd missed a step on the staircase, though neither of us had moved. "Would you like to see it?" I asked.

It was his turn to gape. I caught movement behind him and hurriedly dropped my eyes.

"Pennotdeld," his companion said, coming to the base of the stairs. "What of this delay?"

The red-haired Aldar said something in their own tongue. The other Aldar nodded, though not graciously, and went back down the hall. He turned back to me. "Yes, I wish to see the gown. Later. Come to me."

Later was close to midnight, after I had shut down the tavern in my father's stead, waiting until all the human guests had gone to their rooms. I went to mine briefly, making all the usual noises of my night routine. I didn't undress or uncoil my hair, though I took off my maiden cap. Quietly as I could, I unlatched my bride chest and lifted out the linen-wrapped bundle. Blowing out my candle, I made my way up to the top floor in darkness, by feel alone.

I stood in the hall for what felt like half an hour, clutching the folded dress to my middle. I still didn't know which Aldar had taken which room, and neither one was definitively nicer than the other. The room with more windows overlooked our small garden but was much smaller. The larger room was perpetually dim and overlooked the street. I never had a thought of going back to my room, only a vague puzzlement at how I would explain it, if I chose wrong. Holding my breath, I tried the knob of the larger room. It turned freely. I pushed the door open.

The red-haired Aldar stood by the softly flickering hearth. He looked alert, if not a little startled, as if he had jumped to his feet the second before I entered. He nodded to me and I closed the door quietly behind me.

"Lock it," he said. I hesitated, then did as he said.

I stood at the edge of the rug, still hugging the dress. The Aldar crossed the room, his footsteps silent. He had discarded his boots in favor of soft satin shoes. Somehow, this small change was astoundingly intimate. It made him real in a way that my weeks of longing for him had not. I don't know how I ever mistook him for human. He towered above me, though I'm tall for a woman. His features were all angular, including his ears, which came to a point at the top. Someone once told me that the Aldar disfigured themselves to look that way, but I saw no scars.

He held out his hands and I placed the folded dress in them. His long fingers lifted the linen wrapping, exposing a ruffle of chiffon and a patch of brocade. He traced the pattern for a moment, then handed the bundle back to me. I took it, confused. Was that it? Was that all he wanted? He had not unwrapped it enough to see the design of the dress.

"I wish to see you wear it," he said.

I stared at him. "I would have to undress."

"Do you need my assistance?"

"N-no. I can do it myself."

I contrived a semblance of privacy by drawing the curtains along one side of the bed and stepping behind them. As I untied my leather workaday bodice, I peeked through a gap in the curtains. The Aldar sat in the high-backed chair by the hearth. He put his elbows on the armrests, steepled his hands below his chin, and waited.

"Blood of saints," I whispered to myself. I had not brought the silk chemise or the stays that went under the gown. I would have to wear it directly against my skin. I began to sweat as I struggled to pull the bodice tight behind my back, aware of every second that I made the Aldar wait. I glanced through the slit again. He was pouring the small flagon of fortified wine that I had placed in the room earlier.

At last, the bodice was cinched. I tied the cords, tucked them in, and took a moment to rub my strained shoulders before rounding the corner of the bed. The Aldar looked up at the whisper of cloth over the worn floorboards. He seemed frozen, wine glass hovering half-raised in front of him. Then he said something in his own language and rose, setting the glass aside carefully. It was not one of the vile incantations the elders had warned of. It was an oath, like the words I had muttered to myself as I dressed, a hopeless prayer for resolve when good sense had long fled.

He beckoned me forward. "Come to the light."

Lifting the front of the skirts, I crossed toward the hearth. In the firelight, the silver fabric shimmered like gold. The Aldar circled me, bending to spread the train.

"I would not have thought it possible," he said when he was in front of me once more. He paced away, then turned back, running a hand thoughtfully across his mouth. "I am astonished. Thank you for sharing it with me."

"You're welcome."

"I wonder..." he began. "Would you allow me to show you how an Aldar would arrange it?"

"Please do." In one long stride he was less than an arm's length away from me. I gasped as he put his hands in my hair. In a few quick movements, he removed the wooden clip and shook it free. He separated a lock of hair at my forehead and draped it against my cheek, in front of my ear. My heart pounded, my breath was rapid and shallow. I made a noise between a protest and a sigh when he hooked his fingers under the dress's neckline and pulled the tops of the sleeves down, exposing my shoulders. I had expected the Aldar's touch to be cold, a consequence of his people's reserve and aloofness, but his hands were warm. Trembling, I met his moss green eyes, flecked with amber by the nearby flames. Again, he said something in his language, and glanced down. He pressed his fingers to the bodice, above my breast. I held my breath as he dragged them diagonally past my breast-bone, across the edge of my ribs, to the curve of my waist. Along the trail of his touch, the cloud-like pattern of the brocade glowed, bright as melted steel. Heat surged deep within me.

"Magic," I whispered.

"A simple charm." He crossed the bodice the other direction. My nipples tightened. "The cloth responds to any touch made with pure intention." His hand paused above my navel. "You are bare beneath this."

"I forgot to bring my underpinnings."

He shook his head. "This is how an Aldar would wear it on a special occasion, to display…that is…" He trailed off and didn't appear to have any intention of finishing his sentence. I got the gist.

"Pennotdeld," I said, and he stepped away abruptly. "Is that your name?"

"*Mundin* tongues are troubled by our language. You may call me Penn." He put his hand over his heart, the traditional Aldar greeting. "You are Bel?"

I was surprised he'd remembered my name after over-hearing Lus say it only once, when we first met. "Bel'eva Tagdoma Hombord."

"Beautiful morning, daughter of Tag, people of the boundary," he said, reciting the literal meaning of my names in the ancient tongue. "They name you so that you never forget your loyalties."

He probably meant it as an observation, not a slight, but my stomach plummeted. Being with him was the worst disloyalty I could commit in the eyes of my people. "What does Pennotdeld mean?"

"Troth to the throne."

To be marked for subservience to a monarch seemed far worse than being marked merely by kinship, but I didn't say so. His brows lowered, a crease forming between them.

"I assume the gown achieved your ends?"

"What ends?"

"Was not the ceremony for winning a husband?"

My stomach lurched at the thought of Gabol Mordred. "I would hardly call it winning. It was more like an auction of well-decorated breeding mares."

I took a deep breath to steady myself, but it caught in my throat. Then I was weeping, sinking to the floor as my ribs strained against the seams of the dress. I gasped and gasped.

The tears would not stop. I thought of Gabol's rough grip as we danced, his arm like a bar across my body, preventing my escape. He would never touch me with the reverence that the Aldar—Penn—just had.

"I apologize," he said. I lifted my face from my hands. Penn was beside me on the floor, kneeling on the pooled silk of the dress. "I am not familiar enough with your culture to know how I have offended you."

"You haven't," I said shakily.

Penn unfastened his doublet, pulled out a silk kerchief, and handed it to me. It seemed far too fine for me to wipe my nose on, but I had no choice. It was this or the dress.

"Then what pains you?"

I wiped my face, then balled the kerchief in my fist. How could I explain that my entire world felt wrong? That every lesson I had ever learned felt like a lie? Every achievement somehow a punishment?

"You need not answer." He stood and offered me his hand. "Come."

He brought me to the chair by the hearth and handed me a glass of the fortified wine. I sipped it with my eyes closed, then leaned my head back until my sinuses cleared from my crying. Penn lowered himself to a stool opposite me. Metal flashed from beneath his open doublet.

"You carry knives," I said.

He followed my gaze, then removed the doublet entirely. Over his silk shirt, he wore a leather harness with sheaths fastened under each arm. With a simultaneous flick of both wrists, he liberated the blades. "Daggers," he said. He half-rose and laid the weapons on the table beside us. "All Aldar carry them."

"Are you all soldiers?"

He smiled and a made a noise somewhat like a laugh. "I'm a silk merchant."

My cheeks went hot. Of course. He had sold my father the fabric for the dress. And it explained why his clothes were finer than any I had ever seen before, even on other Aldar. He used his own exquisite form to display his wares.

I touched one of the ornate hilts. The pommel was a falcon's claw clutching a crystal ball. "Why does a textile merchant carry such weapons?"

"My trade is not dangerous in itself. The places it takes me are. When traveling in a hostile land, an Aldar is wise to be armed."

Even knowing what I did of the prejudice against the Aldar, it was hard to imagine coming to Valley Glade and finding its flower-strewn meadows and cottage-lined lanes full of menace. Yet I had seen many humans, from

Councilmen to children, spit at the feet of the Aldar as they passed through the village. Patrons who had come to our tavern without knowing of our unique clientele sometimes took it upon themselves to shout at our Aldar patrons to leave. Given the history of wars between our peoples, it was not hard to imagine such actions turning to violence.

"You do not see me the way other *Mundine* see me." Penn said. "Why is that?"

"You have never given me reason to. No Aldar has. Especially you."

Penn smiled and ran a hand back through his dark red locks. "You like my hair."

I laughed. "How do you know that?"

"You don't always stare at my eyes."

"Well..." I said airily. I folded his kerchief as neatly as I could and placed it on the table, with its embroidered corner bearing a crown and roses facing up. I stood.

"You wish to leave." Penn stood too.

"No," I said. "Even if I did, I'd need help to be free of this dress first."

I stepped toward him and curved my hand around the back of his neck, weaving my fingers into his hair. I drew his face down, close to mine, and kissed him.

The kisses I'd had before were something else—something

lesser—compared to this. Penn's kiss was all-consuming. Hard yet yielding. I opened my mouth for his tongue, groaning as that small part of him entered me. For a long minute we tangled.

When we broke apart for breath, he whispered an Aldarian word harshly. I didn't have to know what it meant to know it was a curse, and not the magical kind. He dug his fingers into the back of my bodice and pulled me against him. I matched his steps as he backed me across the room toward the bed. His lips on mine, I blindly opened the buckles of his dagger harness. He shrugged it off onto the floor, followed shortly by his shirt. I shimmied my arms out of my sleeves and laid my hands on his broad, bare chest. Writhing with impatience as he tugged at my laces, I considered simply lifting my skirts for him instead. Then with a sharp jerk, the back of the bodice came loose. He moved his hands to the front, gripped the busk, and pulled the entire dress over my head in one swift movement.

I was bare before him, except for my stockings. He knelt and undid the ties, rolling the stockings off my feet one after the other. As he stood, he ran his hands up the sides of my calves, my thighs, my waist. I moaned as he came to my breasts and his light caresses roughened. Our mouths came together and he lifted me onto the bed, laying me on my back. He lay beside me, with one leg over mine, and dragged his fingers across my torso, from breast to hip. Again, a pattern of white fire followed his touch.

"How?" I could barely breathe. "I don't understand."

"I wonder…" Penn said, in huskier tones than he had before. He slid off the bed, then grasped my hips and took me with him. Our feet on the floor again, he turned me toward the long mirror. Standing behind me, he slowly dragged his fingers over my ribs, between my breasts, circled my taut nipples. Everywhere his fingers went, the pattern of curling clouds followed.

"A lingering charm," he said. "Nothing more."

Curls of light followed his hand down to my navel. The heat between my thighs turned into a deep ache of need. I pressed myself back against his chest and hips. He kissed along my neck and plunged his hand lower. Then the fire was within me, pulsing brighter and brighter under his touch. I gasped into his hair, which had fallen loose over his shoulder.

"Look," he said, turning my face toward the mirror with his free hand. "Look."

As each crest of pleasure clenched my body, ripples and spirals of light danced across my skin, arching up my chest, to my neck, shining brightest where Penn pressed his lips against my cheek. Then I was completely lost, aware of nothing but his touch. When I opened my eyes again, I turned in his arms and kissed him fiercely.

"I want more of you," I said.

He kissed me back, then drew his face away. "You do not fear breeding?"

"No," I said, determined not to seem jarred by his directness, nor the hard press of his lust against my middle. "No, I fear to have my will taken from me. I fear a life that is not my own." I put my hand between us, stroking him. "This…this night can be mine. I do not fear it."

In seconds, we were back on the bed. He shed his breeches and stockings before climbing over me. Everywhere our skin touched sparked like an ember. He eased open my thighs. I rolled my hips, eager, needful.

"Please," I said. "Penn."

He shushed me and kissed my ear. "Tonight we have no names." And he entered me.

I cried out, mostly in surprise at the new sensation of being stretched, filled. But he was gentle, moving slowly until he was sure I could bear more. And I wanted more. More until the boundaries between us disappeared. More until I could feel him at the tip of every nerve. More until we were both left shuddering and dazed, stretched out on the rumpled blankets.

After a while, he rose and carefully folded my gown back into its linen wrappings. He brought me more wine without letting me rise from the bed. I felt the heavy hand of sleep beckoning to me. Penn donned a dressing robe—silk, of course—and watched as I dressed sluggishly.

"I return to Aldar lands tomorrow," he said as I pinned my hair.

"Oh. When will you be back?" *Please let it be before my Initiation a month from now*, I pleaded silently.

"I am not sure." He rose from the edge of the bed and walked me to the door. He slipped the bolt free. "Most likely my trade will bring me here again. And I will return to claim the child, if there is one."

"The child," I repeated, a cold trickle of horror running through me. I hugged the bundled dress against me as I had before I first entered his room. "No, you can't. I will be married by then. Any child I bear will belong to my husband."

He stared at me as if I were a fool. "No child of mine would belong to a human."

"Not by blood, no. But by our laws, any child born to a woman belongs to her husband, no matter by whom it is gotten."

"Our laws say differently."

"This is an argument over something that does not exist," I said, "There are no half-Aldar children."

"No there aren't." Penn's fists clenched at his sides. "Not anymore. Your people made sure of that."

"What are you talking about?"

"Do they not teach you of the last war?"

"Of course they do."

"But not the reason for it."

Though I had never questioned it before this moment, I knew what I was about to say was a lie. I said it anyway. "Border disputes."

"No," Penn said, his voice grave and low. "Murder of hundreds of children, and many of the parents who dared to bring them into the world."

I shook my head, tears burning in my eyes. "That can't be true. They can't have killed children. They wouldn't."

"Not 'they,' Bel. You. Your people." He opened the door. "Please leave."

I didn't leave. I fled.

Penn and his blond companion departed at the break of dawn. I watched their carriage leave, then donned my apron and rushed to clean his room. Both wine glasses had been wiped clean, as if they'd never been used. The bed covers were folded back, the sheets unstained, ready to be laundered. Not even my sharp-eyed mother would have found evidence of our tryst. I should have felt relieved, but I felt hollow.

Weeks passed, and I began to fear a different kind of evidence. One day, I took a bite of the sausages and potatoes Egold had made and had to spit them right out.

"You got ash in the pot," I said.

"No I didn't," Egold said.

"Taste this." I handed him my fork.

He chewed and shrugged. "Same as always. Just because I'm blind doesn't mean I don't know my way around the kitchen. I'll thank you not to accuse me otherwise."

Baffled, I took another bite. The food was grainy and bitter on my tongue. Only by washing it down with tea did I manage to clear the plate. Each successive meal was worse. It didn't matter what I ate, it was all the same. After a few days, I could only eat biscuits, and even those I only kept down half the time. Water tasted foul. I thought a rat had fallen down our well, but neither of my parents could taste it.

I kept silent after that. I knew the signs well enough. I hid my sickness, forcing myself to eat and cautiously discarding whatever my stomach later rejected. Soon I would not be able to hide. My mother would notice the absence of blood in my linens. She almost found me out sooner, when she caught me in her apothecary, searching deep in the back shelves.

I jumped up when she came to the door, and she gave a startled shout. "Bel'eva! I thought we had a burglar."

"Don't worry," I said as brightly as I could manage. "It was locked securely. I borrowed the key."

My false cheer did not reassure her. She raised her brows and lowered her voice. "Bel'eva, why are you holding a jar of rue?"

"Rue?" I repeated, squinting at the label. "Oh, I meant to get the anise."

My mother set down her candle and put the back of her hand to my cheek. "Are you feeling unwell?"

"My stomach is upset," I said truthfully.

"Let me brew you a remedy." She took the jar of rue from me and retrieved the anise from the shelf. The two containers looked nothing alike. As we left the apothecary, my mother slipped the jar of rue into her pocket. I knew I would not find it again.

Her anise remedy helped me eat one small meal, but I was in despair. The memory of my night with the Aldar was meant to be the last good thing I had that was truly mine. It had morphed into this horrible secret instead. I did not dare tell Lus. Anytime I had mentioned the Aldar to her, either Penn or his people in general, she had recoiled. So I let her believe that my worry, my sadness, had to do with dreading my wedding to Gabol Mordred. My two plights were inextricable, after all. I feared what Gabol would do when he found out he hadn't married a virgin.

I resolved to delay discovery for as long as I could. At the end of a shift in the tavern, I hid a kitchen knife in my skirts. In my bed, I lifted my chemise, exposing the inside of my thigh. Yet every time I came close to pressing the blade to my leg, the world spun. After half a dozen attempts, I vomited into my chamber pot and gave up. I hid the knife under my pillow and decided to try again the next night.

I woke in the morning to dampness between my legs. I flung back the covers to discover a smear of crimson. Disoriented, I wondered if I had cut myself in my sleep. I lifted my pillow. The knife was still there, perfectly clean. Amidst my now constant hunger, thirst, and dizziness, my abdomen ached. I curled around the pain and cried.

My blood came and went, but I did not get better. I worked or napped during mealtimes so no one would notice how little I ate. I walked slowly to hide my dizziness and chose tasks that didn't require me to lift anything heavy. One afternoon, my father patted me on the shoulder and my knees nearly buckled.

"Bring the Aldar more ale," he said. "I have to get the pork from the butcher."

I nodded, gripping the edge of the bar to stay upright. How long had Penn been there, without me noticing? He was alone this time. It took all my concentration to keep my hand from shaking as I put the full mug of ale down on his table. He said nothing. He pretended I wasn't there, just as he was supposed to.

I did my best to ignore him too, but the longer we didn't acknowledge each other, the more I felt like screaming. I watched the other patrons instead. As usual, they took turns glaring in Penn's direction, muttering amongst themselves. A series of horrible questions surfaced in my mind. What if there was some truth to their prejudice? What if the elders were right? What if Penn had cursed me?

Trying to shake off the thoughts only made me queasy. What reason could he have to harm me? Did he believe that if we had made a child, I would have kept it away from him? I had implied as much by telling him of our laws. Was that enough for him to wish me illness and death?

After an hour, Penn stacked some coins on the table and left. Abandoning the busy tavern, I followed him. Out in the side yard, he had led his horse from the stable and was checking the saddle.

"Stop, Aldar," I said.

He spun, one hand inside his doublet. He sighed with relief when he saw me. Glancing around, he strode quickly to me. Touching my shoulder, he drew me under the overhang of a shed, where no one coming from the tavern or the street would immediately see us.

"Penn, something is wrong," I said. I felt a flicker of shame at the tight threat of tears I could hear in my own voice. "What have you done to me?"

Penn held up his hands. "I have done nothing to you."

I shook my head. Taking my maidenhood was hardly nothing, but that wasn't something he did to me. We had done it together. Penn took a breath as if to speak, then didn't.

"But I'm terribly ill," I said. "At first, I thought there would be a child. Then I was reassured there wouldn't be." I swallowed my mortification at sharing this detail with him. "Yet I continue to feel strange. Dizzy, weak. I have no appetite at all…"

"You think I have laid a spell on you." Penn's eyes narrowed to green slits. He corrected his posture, becoming stiff. "That is what you have been taught of my people, of Aldar men. We are sorcerers, base magicians who deceive and seduce and enthrall with foul forces that you do not understand, but think your saints can protect you from."

I felt an odd mix of disgust and defensiveness at his words, even though they were gentler than many human descriptions I'd heard of the Aldar. Not merely sorcerers, they were dark creatures, beholden to hell, instruments of demons if not demons themselves. Despite hearing such things many times, I never believed them. Surely he knew that if I did, I would not have lain with him. Lain…as if what we did had been anything like repose. As if I hadn't wrapped my legs around him, pulling him in, deep and hard against my core. Even now, standing tall and rigid with anger, he looked glorious. Lust and anger flooded me together.

"If you have a nervous condition, it is no fault of mine." Penn's voice remained cold.

"It is not a nervous condition. Food tastes like ash, water like mildew. The earth moves beneath my feet every few steps. When I sleep, I feel like the bed is tumbling on the sea. I'll waste away before long."

"I did not curse you, Bel!"

"Then what is wrong with me?"

"I am not particularly familiar with *Mundin* afflictions. If I had known you had such fragile constitutions, I would not have…" He shrugged his cloak closed and fastened the silver clip at the base of his neck. "I cannot help you. Go see one of your doctors. Or perhaps one of your holy women."

I caught a fistful of the suede cloth and kept him from stepping away. "To tell them what? That I let a devil inside me and—"

Penn's eyes blazed. I hadn't meant to call him a devil. I'd meant to argue how useless a priestess's help would be. But the damage was done. "Yes," he said. "Go plead for an exorcism. Rid yourself of me."

I shoved him away. "Damn you."

"Am I not already damned in your eyes?"

In a flash of red hair and silver cloth, he mounted his horse and was gone, leaving me trembling. The tavern door opened behind me.

"Oh, it's you, Bel," my father said, taking in the empty yard. "I heard your voice and thought some patrons had grown rowdy out here."

I blinked at him and picked up a basket of rags I had taken down from the line earlier.

"Are you alone?" he asked.

"I am."

"I heard another voice. A man."

I shook my head, donned a liar's smile. "Must have been Egold humming."

My affliction made the days blend together. Midsummer arrived, the day of Initiation. My mother was beside herself trying to improve my looks. She rubbed animal fat mixed with lavender oil into my face, desperate to fake a healthy glow on my skin. It had become papery and thin, especially around my eyes. In the end, she resorted to staining my lips with berry juice. Like everything else, it tasted bitter.

Draped over my thin limbs, my white Initiation cloak gave me the look of a walking corpse. I felt like one. Thank goodness we had rehearsed the Oaths of Initiation when I was still healthy. If I had tried to learn them in the last few weeks, none of it would have stuck. My mind had become a sieve. My only comfort was Lus, who held me by the elbow, steadying me until we were instructed to take our places in the nave of the Sacred House.

Like at the Fete of Choosing, families took their places on either side of the hall, this time joined by their sons, our betrothed. I spotted Gabol in the crowd. He stared at me, but not covetously. It was either disgust or confusion that curled his lip. I did not look like the same girl he'd selected to be his wife.

As the high priestess, Lady Mordred once again presided.

She sat in an ornate wooden chair in the apse. The ceremony began as she unhooked the heavy chain from her neck and draped it over her lap, so the holy amulet hung from her knee. In the assigned order, maidens in white cloaks and veils kneeled before her and repeated their Oaths of Initiation, kissing the amulet after each one. Isabet, Nadey, Ulra, Lus, Yana. Then me.

When I knelt before Lady Mordred, I swayed. I knew I would not have the strength to stand back up on my own.

"Bel'eva Tagdoma Hombord, do you pledge yourself to the continuance of this holy house?"

"Yes, I pledge myself to the continuance of this holy house," I murmured, and kissed the amulet.

"Do you swear your fealty to the congregation here gathered?"

"Yes, I swear my fealty to the congregation here gathered," I pledged. Even after so many lips, the amulet was still cold.

"Do you hold the saints in your heart, worshipping no others?"

I pledged and kissed.

"Will you uphold the saints' holy laws above any other laws?"

I pledged and kissed.

"Do you come from your father's house in honor and in faith?"

I pledged and kissed.

"Do you come to your betrothed as a virgin, in purity untouched?"

I froze. I had forgotten about this oath. Until now my voice had been quiet, only loud enough so that Lady Mordred could hear me.

"No."

The word echoed through the chamber, high into the mosaiced ceiling, along the pews, to the rosette windows above the entrance. The families nearest the front and the remaining girls in line gasped. The amulet jerked from my hand.

"What did you say?"

I met her milky blue eyes. "No, I am not a virgin."

Lady Mordred rose and lurched away, as if afraid she might catch the rot she now perceived on my soul. The crowd grew uproarious with shock and confusion. Gabol rushed out of the pews, followed closely by his parents and mine. Holy Thralls rushed to herd the remaining maidens into an antechamber, away from the scene of scandal.

"What is the meaning of this?" my father demanded.

Lady Mordred stared at me. "She has refused an Oath."

"Bel'eva!" My mother turned my name into a scold.

"Which one?" my father asked.

"The Oath of Purity," Lady Mordred said.

"She has not been well," my mother said. "She's weak and confused. Repeat the Oath, and she will pledge it."

"She told me she is not a virgin," Lady Mordred said. "Unless I heard incorrectly."

Their faces turned to me, still kneeling below them. I stared at the priestess and said, "I have known a man."

My mother wailed. Rather overdramatically, I thought. She had probably suspected the truth ever since she caught me in her apothecary. Gabol's parents gasped. Their son blanched and said, "Blood of saints," then yelped as Lady Mordred started to beat him with the amulet.

"You horrid, corrupt, sinful boy!" Lady Mordred screeched.

"Ah, ah! Auntie, it wasn't me!" Gabol shrank from the priestess's assault. "It wasn't me!"

"I knew it!" Gabol's father pointed at mine. "I knew that tavern was a brothel!"

"How dare you!" My father took a step toward him and my mother wailed again.

"Alright, I might have taken a sip," Gabol said, as his aunt's arm began to tire. "But that was a long time ago and I never finished the bottle!"

I need not have worried whether I would be able to stand back up on my own. My parents dragged me from the Sacred House through the transom door, various Mordreds hollering after us. They dragged me up to our apartments, past a very startled Egold. Only my mother flinging herself over me kept my father from stripping me to my waist and whipping me.

"No! You cannot mark her. This can be fixed! You must not ruin her further."

The leather flogging whip creaked in my father's fists. "How?"

"Increase her dowry. Give Mordred a stake in the tavern."

"He thinks it's a whorehouse!" He slapped the whip against his own hand.

"The boy who did this. He can trade brides with Gabol. It has been done before."

Through the tails of my mother's matron veil, I watched my father pacing. At length he nodded, setting the whip aside. My mother rose and helped me to the divan. They stood above me, side by side.

"Bel'eva," my mother said, "who sullied you?"

I kept my mouth closed and shook my head.

"If you do not tell us," my father said, "we cannot save you."

"Tag!" My mother grabbed his shirt. "She's our only child!"

The punishment for whoredom was imprisonment, for a term determined by the Council. Release was possible, but only into lifelong servitude as an Unseen in a Sacred House.

My mother clutched my shoulders. "Who was it? Did Gabol lie?"

I shook my head.

"Was it Egold?"

I shook my head again, trying not to smile at the absurdity of the question. Egold was devout. The idea of taking my maidenhood would have horrified him.

"What about Egold?" My mother said speculatively to my father. "If she will not tell us which boy, Egold doesn't have a wife—"

"I will not spoil the blood of my clan with that of a peasant," my father said. "If she will not tell us, someone else will. Vile affairs like this are never truly secret."

I smiled at this. The only person who had seen Penn and me near each other, who might have heard us together, was Penn's blond Aldar companion. Even if he had been here, it would never occur to my parents to question an Aldar. No matter what happened to me, no matter what punishment was chosen, my secret would still be mine.

They took me to my room and locked the door. In the coming days, they brought me food. I barely tried to eat, though I drank the water. Mostly I slept. I was so weak that the rocking dizziness of the bed did not bother me much. Then one afternoon, they flung Lus into the room. My parents and Lady Mordred followed.

Lus's round eyes were red from crying. "Bel, I'm sorry!" I got up on my knees on the bed and she stumbled into my arms. "I'm so sorry. They whipped me. They threatened to whip Eget, too, and he's done nothing!"

"Let your daughter deny the accusations of Eget's wife," Lady Mordred said.

"Eget's wife," I said as my father took Lus by the arm and dragged her away from me. She covered her mouth with her hands, tears streaming down her face. My dearest friend had already been wed, and I was not there. Suddenly, I saw the selfishness of what I had done. "I'm sorry, Lus."

She shook her head and let out a coughing sob.

"Say again what you said beneath your father's whip," Lady Mordred said to Lus.

"I witnessed Bel speaking with an Aldar," Lus said.

The world rocked and swayed beneath me. *No, please no.*

"If Bel has been sullied, it is because she was under his spell," Lus said.

"Is this true?" Lady Mordred asked me. Beside her, my parents awaited my answer with pleading expressions. Disgust welled up inside me, creating a sour lump in my throat.

"There was no spell," I said. "I went to him willingly."

My father lurched forward, unclasping his belt from his waist. Both my mother and Lus screamed as he pushed me down on the bed and whipped my back and arms.

"Tag Hombord!" Lady Mordred shouted. My father fell back, huffing. "The saints will punish this whore. You need not debase yourself in the attempt." She turned to Lus. "You may go, Lady Floriz."

Lus backed out of the room, shaking her head as she stared at me. My mother was in a heap. My father hauled her up by the elbow.

"Do not waste your tears," he said.

Then they were gone, the door slamming behind them, the key turning in the lock. I fell back on the bed, gasping. I was lucky that I was fully dressed when they came, and that my father had only had his belt. The welts stung, but none had broken skin.

I was too tired to cry. Too tired to curse Lus's name. Too tired to do anything but lie there and think about how quickly I had turned from a prized daughter into a befouled whore. If they could do this to me, one of their own, I could see how they could do it to others, those they viewed as lesser. I saw the path between their abhorrence of me to the murder of children. What Penn had told me—what my people had done—it was true.

Darkness fell. I drifted in and out of sleep. A breeze ruffled my hair. The window was open. I was sure my father had barred the shutters from the outside. I sat up. A sharp-shouldered shadow moved toward me.

At first, I thought it was Gabol in his Academy uniform. I shrank against the headboard. The shadow moved closer. There was a clatter and a light appeared in its hand, illuminating the gray wool jerkin and cap of a town guard. And his face.

"Penn!"

"Quiet," he hissed.

"Oh, saints alive! Oh saints, what have you done?"

"I climbed along your neighbor's roof and came through the window."

"No, to your hair!"

He set down the lantern and took off his cap, revealing his bright red hair, cropped short in the human style. I scrambled forward on my knees and touched the shorn locks. My eyes filled with tears.

"You look terrible," I said.

"It will grow back, Bel."

"I don't mean that," I studied his face between my hands. He had bags under his eyes and his cheekbones stood out more than they had before. "Are you ill?"

"Maybe. In a way," he said. He spotted the welts on my arm and pulled away. I let him examine me, run his hands along my bony limbs. He said a curse, the same word he'd said right after I first kissed him. This time it was full of pain, not lust. "How long have they imprisoned you here?"

"Less than a week, I think. I have not been well since I last saw you."

"You've wasted away," he said softly. He pulled me into his lap and I clung to him. "I'm so sorry I did not listen. You asked for my help and I did not listen."

I kissed his forehead, his cheek, the pointed tip of his ear. "I was awful and ignorant."

"But not entirely without wisdom," he said. "I have been unwell since I left you. Everything you told me…tasteless food, putrid water, the tilting earth…all of it has befallen me too. I went to my mother. She took me to her Royal Enchantress, who said her incantations, tasted my blood. Strong magic has taken hold of me. To know if it is a curse, all who are afflicted must be tested."

Before I had met him, I had suspected that magic was yet another of the elders' lies to keep people in line, a threat they could point to. I tried to process all he had just told me. "She tasted your blood? Why a *Royal* Enchantress? Wait—you told your mother about me?"

"No, it would not be safe to tell her about you. And only a Royal Enchantress could be entrusted with knowing that a member of the royal family might be cursed."

"What in heaven are you talking about? I thought you were a silk merchant."

He squinted at me as if trying to figure out if I was joking. I continued to look at him blankly. "I am…but I'm also the third child of Heima, Queen of the Aldar."

"As in…all the Aldar?"

Penn laughed and it sent tingles along my nerves. "I should think my heritage was obvious." He tugged at a lock of hair curling over his forehead. "They truly do not teach you anything of our people, do they? Only Aldar in the royal line have red hair. It's been so for a century or more. That is why I said the dress made you look like an Aldar princess."

"Because you're a prince."

"Because you have red hair, too."

That I had resembled royalty in his eyes was almost as unfathomable as me unwittingly making love to a member of the Aldar royal family. Now that I knew what he was, I realized the clues had been there. When he told me the meaning of his name—troth to the throne—I'd assumed it meant he served the throne, not that he was in the line of succession. Then there was the monogram of the crown and roses on his kerchief, the ease with which he gave commands, the unusual fineness of his clothes. The blond Aldar he sometimes traveled with did not dress as grandly as he did, though they were supposedly in the same business.

"I thought the other Aldar was your employer."

"Jerrovel?" Penn laughed again and heat pulsed within me. "He's the son of the royal steward and my business partner. He speaks for me with certain clients who need to be impressed by the silent presence of the crown." His face turned serious. He glanced around the room. "I assume that you told your parents about me."

"Not willingly." I swallowed hard, thinking of Lus. "I was betrayed."

"Tell me you did not give them my name."

"We had no names. Remember?"

Penn grabbed me and kissed me hard. He was less gentle this time, but I did not want gentleness. Wrapped in his arms, with him moving deep inside me, I felt my strength returning. Seeking a release from the pain we had endured, we moved almost frantically, until we had to stifle our cries and collapsed, shaking, against each other. I slept for a while with my head on his chest, the bed remarkably steady beneath us. I woke to him stroking my hair.

"How did you know to find me here?" I asked, kissing his chin.

"Tavern gossip can be profoundly informative."

I sat up. "You were downstairs? They'll be interrogating any Aldar they can find!"

"Good thing there were no Aldar to be found." He grabbed the guardsman's cap and put it on, showing me how it covered the tops of his ears.

"You could have been killed."

"I have my daggers."

One man against a horde of drunken bigots bent on revenge…I shook my head. His daggers would only delay his death, not prevent it.

"We need to flee," Penn said, as if reading my thoughts. "Before sunrise."

"But the curse…I'm too weak to stand, let alone run." My heart dropped. "You must go without me."

Penn shook his head. "You did not hear what these men said they would do to you. No prison or Sacred House will keep you safe." He paused. "They are calling you my whore."

I was not surprised, but it was clear that hearing me called that name had pained him. "I don't know what to do," I admitted.

"The Enchantress told me how to call forth the mark of the curse, if there is one," Penn said. "Once we know what it is, we may be able to break it." He held up his hand in front of him, the back of it facing me. "Put your palm against mine." I did as he said. "Repeat these words. You do not need to know what they mean." He slowly said something in Aldarian. I repeated the best I could. "Now we say them together."

We started the incantation again. A glow emerged from between our hands. Bolts of light shot up both our arms. A sound began, a great rumbling that shook the bed beneath us, the other furniture, the very walls.

I broke off speaking and whispered, "Stop, stop." When I pulled my hand from Penn's there was resistance, like invisible glue had been spread between our palms. We sat in frozen silence for a long time, desperately listening for sounds of stirring in the rest of the building.

"They cannot find you here with me," I said. "They would kill you where you stand."

"If I leave without breaking the curse, you will die," Penn countered. "Is there anywhere close by where we could complete the incantation without being overheard?"

I thought first of the tavern cellar, then of the catacombs beneath the Sacred House. But not only the dead slept there, the Unseen—excommunicated servants of the priestess— slept there too. Then I had a flash of inspiration.

"The fortress on the mount," I said. "It's not an easy path, but I know the way. Even in the dark, I wager."

"Take us there. Now."

Oddly enough, when I rose to put on my shoes and my cloak, my legs were steady. While I gathered a few useful items, Penn opened my bride chest and unwrapped my Choosing gown. With one of his daggers, he cut the seams that tacked the bodice to the skirt and rolled it up.

"Why are you taking that?"

"I don't know," he said. "It feels too important to leave behind." I suspected he was being sentimental. He stuffed the bodice into his satchel, then helped me up onto the dresser and out the window. The night was balmy. Not everyone in the village was asleep, though it was well past midnight. Every scrape of our shoes across the neighbor's roof tiles made my heart pound faster. Penn hopped down from the roof. He caught me easily when I jumped after him; his reach was higher than the eaves. I led us through the shadowy parts of the village, choosing alleys over streets.

"She does excellent work, you know," Penn said as we passed Widow Cork's cobbler's shop. I smiled at the reference to our first meeting and paused long enough to kiss him vehemently.

We went a mile and I still hadn't stumbled or felt dizzy. I wasn't even winded after we swam across the river, nor as we climbed the twisting path through the glen to the fortress. Once we were inside the walls, Penn took the lead.

"There should be a sunken chamber this way," he said, holding up the half-shuttered lantern, with its oddly cool glow. He'd explained it was a fairy light, not a candle, that burned inside it.

"Have you been here before?" I asked. He shook his head. "How do you know your way around the rooms of this fortress?"

"The arrangement of Aldar castles are mostly the same, even through the centuries. The *Mundin* touches here have not changed the structure much."

"This is not an Aldar castle."

He paused and turned, the lantern's dim glow between us. "Our peoples built this place together, in times of peace."

I looked around at what I could see of the broken walls, skeletal stairways, and rain-rounded stones. "I had no idea. They never told us who built it."

"Division only thrives in ignorance."

I followed him into what had been the large open courtyard at the center of the fortress, then stopped in my tracks.

"What is that wonderful smell?" Following my nose, I came to a plant with small red berries nestled amongst the stones. They looked familiar, so I popped one into my mouth. Sweetness exploded on my tongue and I groaned. "What kind of berries are these?" I asked, stuffing more of them into my mouth.

Penn brought the lantern and cocked his head at me. "Those are strawberries."

"They're like no strawberries I've ever tasted. Do you think the soil here is enchanted?"

"I do not think so," Penn said. He ate a berry and made a noise of surprise. "Hold on."

He fished through his satchel and handed me a biscuit. Tentatively, I took a bite. Rich, nutty, buttery goodness flooded my senses. I ate the entire thing in two more bites, then gracelessly licked the crumbs from my fingers. "Heavens, that's glorious. Is all Aldar food that good?"

"Bel, that was hard tack," he said. "I stole it from the guard house when I took this uniform." He took out another piece and took a bite, then made a noise of such profound pleasure that I almost tackled him. "You're right. This is delicious.

But I suspect that it is we who have changed, not the food."

We shared his canteen, which as far as I could tell was full of nectar, then continued through the ruins. We came to a broad stairway that led to an ancient meeting hall, lower than the rest of the floors by the height of a man. On the only part of the old floor that had not been overtaken by dirt and grass, I found a mosaic. A rose, very much like the ones on Penn's kerchief, gleamed at the center, its stem crossed by a sword. I recognized the sword's flared blade and curved cross-guard: a carving of it adorned Lady Mordred's holy amulet.

"This inlay has both Aldar and human symbols," I said. "You were right."

"Of course I was," Penn said, though not defensively. He was merely perplexed that I had doubted it. He stepped onto the face of the rose. "Come."

He raised his hand and I put my palm against his again. He reminded me of the Aldarian words, and we said them together. A light as bright as the sun burst from between our hands. There was no heat, only tingling, as jets of light went up my arm. Around us, the walls trembled, desiccated mortar turned to dust, loose stones tumbled free. Just when I began to worry the fortress might come down on top of us, Penn said a final Aldarian word on his own, and the rumbling stopped. The light disappeared. He put his free hand on my wrist and pulled our palms apart. Then he tore off my cloak and started to unhook the front of my dress.

"Penn, I don't think this is the time for…"

"Look," he said, touching my exposed chest. When he moved his hand, it revealed a glowing brand. Two triangular runes, corners overlapping, were seared painlessly into the skin atop my breastbone. "This is far more dire than I thought. We're lucky to be alive after so much time."

Penn stumbled back and sat on a half-crumbled stair. My heart jumped in fear.

"Who did this to us?"

"We did," he said. "It's not a curse. It's a soul bond."

"What does that mean?"

He took off his cap and rubbed his face. His red hair looked purple in the moonlight. "It means you're in love with me."

A thrill went through me. My eyes burned. But I scoffed. "That's absurd."

He shook his head. "Not only that." He unhooked his doublet and untied the collar of his shirt. The same glowing brand appeared on his chest. "It means I am in love with you."

"What?"

"Ancient magic does not lie," he said, closing his shirt over the mark. I stared at the subtle illumination beneath the silk.

"How do we break it?" I asked.

He looked stricken. "You wish to?"

"Won't we die otherwise?"

"A soul bond is an unbreakable magic covenant between mates. It only becomes a curse when it is resisted, when the two souls are kept apart. That is why we became ill."

"I don't understand. How could something like this happen between a human and an Aldar? We barely know each other."

"One might have any number of potential mates, but only one bond can ever be made. It only happens if the two are already in love before they…" He said a word in Aldarian that was more elegant than any I could think of for it.

"We did this," I said, sinking onto the stair beside him.

He brushed my hair behind my ear. "I am sorry."

"You're sorry!" I caught his hand. "I started this, remember?" One distracted moment…and now I was a ruined maiden, on the run with an Aldar prince.

"I believe if you had not, I would have." He twined his fingers through mine.

I rested my head against his shoulder. The glass-less windows of the hall faced east, revealing a subtle gloaming above the horizon.

"Bel'eva," Penn said, and I knew he was not merely saying my name.

"We cannot stay here," I said.

"You do not wish to break the bond?"

"I thought we couldn't."

"There is one way." He reached into his open doublet and took out a dagger. He held it with the point aimed at his heart and met my eyes. "You would be free. You could go across the world and never suffer from the distance."

"What in heaven is the matter with you?" I asked, snatching the dagger from him. The Aldar were known for their reserve. I decided they also had a penchant for melodrama. My Aldar did, anyway. I reached under his arm and returned the blade to its sheath. "Besides, I would likely die regardless." He blinked at me, green eyes dark in the moonlight. "Because I do love you and I do not wish to be parted from you."

He kissed me, then nuzzled his face in my hair and murmured something in his language. This time, I knew exactly what it meant.

The glow to the east had grown into a soft arch of violet. I stood and retrieved my cloak.

"Will we go north?" I asked. "To your people's lands?"

"They are no more likely to accept our union than your people are." I let the weight of that knowledge settle into me. Neither of us would be able to go home again. "I have associates at the ports in whom we might put our trust."

"Might?"

"It is better than the surety that your people will torture and kill us."

I resisted the instinct to argue against this, recalling the sharp fire of my father's belt, and his whip many times before that. My mother had never intervened to save me from suffering, only to preserve my skin so that I'd make a more appealing bride. I wished I could say someone would stand for us, but even Lus had betrayed me, albeit under duress. She had never handled pain well. I knew I was leaving her behind to endure even more of it.

"Wait," I said as we began to make our way back through the fortress. I climbed to the window ledge facing north where Lus and I often sat. I took the wooden clip from my hair and tucked it into a crevice in the rock. Someday, I hoped Lus would find it, and know that I had left without any hate for her in my heart.

We descended the mount to the river and stole a rowboat from a farmer's rickety dock. With the current in our favor and the strokes of Penn's long arms at the oars, we came to the marshy delta when the morning was still rosy and new. We paused in the tall grass to fashion me a makeshift matron's veil out of a corner cut from one of my petticoats. It was a thin disguise, but if anyone was pursuing us, they'd be looking for a maiden, not a married woman.

The port town of Caluba sat on a wedge of land between the marsh and a sandy bay. Penn clearly knew his way around the streets, but he was a bit at a loss for where to go. A tavern on the high road would mean hiding in plain sight, a strategy that appealed to him. But the establishments down by the docks were more accustomed to foreigners, so we would not stand out as much. We stood near a fruit-seller's stall, debating our choices between heavenly bites of melon and orange.

"Bel'eva!"

The shout came from ahead of us. I froze. Penn didn't. He shoved me behind him with one hand and reached for a dagger with the other. The fruit he'd been eating hit the ground with a dusty smack. Through the crook of his arm, I saw a man running toward us.

"Come no closer," Penn said. The man stopped. I gripped Penn's elbow.

"You can't draw a weapon in the street!" I whispered frantically. "It's a crime."

"Add it to the lot," Penn muttered.

"You would oblige me by unhanding my cousin, brother," the man said. Recognition rattled through me, as well as relief that he'd addressed Penn as a fellow human.

"Alfez?" I peeked from behind Penn's shoulder. It had been years since I'd seen the grandson of my father's uncle, the man my mother had said was without honor. The family resemblance was strong, despite his uncommon attire. He was tall, dressed in a bright smock of blue and green that no one from Valley Glade would have been caught dead in. His strawberry blond hair almost as long as Penn's had been.

"Saints alive, Bel'eva, what are you doing here?" Alfez relaxed, even though Penn still had his hand on his dagger under his doublet.

"State whether you are friend or foe, or do not speak to her again," Penn said.

I shook off Penn's grip and stepped out from behind him. "He doesn't have to. My parents hate him. I think that says enough."

Alfez's eyes widened, but he smiled. "You've come a long way since the brat who used to leave toads in my bed." He looked Penn up and down. "In more ways than one. Come, we should not talk in the street. The less time people have to figure out what you are, the better."

Penn stiffened. I took his hand, practically dragging him the first few steps after my cousin. Alfez led us down a lane to a stone cottage on the edge of town.

"I imagine you're hungry, if you've come all the way from Valley Glade in one night," he said, ushering us inside.

If I hadn't been hungry before, the smells inside the cottage made me ravenous. Sizzling pork, fried eggs, something sweet and buttery, something rich and nutty. Alfez called out something I didn't quite catch. Penn stared at him in astonishment. Then both of us stared at the tremendously tall woman who appeared in the doorway from another room, brushing icy hair back over her shoulder.

"This is my wife, Idrigaina," Alfez said. "My dear, this is my cousin Bel'eva and…sorry, I didn't catch your name."

Idrigaina gasped and dropped to one knee in front of Penn. "Your Highness."

"Oh, well, I say." Alfez raised his eyebrows at me. "That's interesting."

Penn bent over and laid his hands on Idrigaina's shoulders, saying something quietly. She got to her feet again, smiling.

"You're married to an Aldar," I said, as if that wasn't painfully obvious.

"Apparently, it's a proclivity that runs in the family," Alfez said, looking between my matron's veil and Penn.

"Oh, actually…" I snatched the veil off my head.

"I'm sure it's quite a story," Alfez said. "Tell it to us over tea."

We told them everything in a cozy sitting room overlooking the sea, Idrigaina plying us with ever more delicious foods and drinks. At one point I felt so full I thought I was going to be sick. Instead, I leaned back into the cushions of their divan. Penn draped his arm over my shoulders, as if he'd done so many times before. I struggled not to cry with happiness, reminding myself that we were hardly out of harm's way yet.

"I don't understand how you do it," I said to my cousin and his wife. "Living in the open. Penn told me the last war was fought over the mixing of peoples."

Idrigaina nodded. "The ports are not under your King's eye as much as places further inland. If he watched the ports too closely, enforced the laws too strictly, his coffers would suffer. His agents turn a blind eye to almost everything that goes on here."

"As for the Sacred Order," Alfez said. "Their tolerance is closely tied to coin." He gestured around the cottage. "As you can see, we live simply. I would be a much richer man if it weren't for the tributes I pay in the name of the saints."

"What of the other *Mundine*?" Penn asked. "Do you not live in constant fear of a torchlit mob coming for you in the night?"

Idrigaina and Alfez looked unsettled by his question, then the Aldar woman shrugged. "We only live here in the summer. The rest of the year, we make our home across the sea, in the Southunder. No one is bothered by us there."

They shared their story with us. It was not so dissimilar from ours. They had met when Alfez saved Idrigaina from a mob much like the one Penn described. Feeling herself indebted, she had offered him her maidenhead as a reward, believing it was what humans valued most. But Alfez refused her offer and asked her to let him court her instead. Not long after, she accepted his hand. They fled by night from his home village of Woodmere, near the northern border. At the port city of Bargolan, some thirty miles south of Caluba, they found a sympathetic priest, who agreed to marry them.

"He's still there," Alfez said. "In his tiny Sacred Chapel. We send him a crate of gifts every year when we come back from the continent."

"I do not doubt he would be willing to do the same favor again," Idrigaina said. "His grandmother was an Aldar. Nearly two entire generations of his family were wiped out in the purging."

Penn abruptly lifted his arm from my shoulders. He said something to Idrigaina in Aldarian, and she stood quickly and retrieved one of his daggers, which he'd set aside while his stolen jerkin and my cloak dried by the hearth.

"Stand up, cousin," Alfez said to me.

Still perplexed as to what was happening, I stood. Penn slid to the floor on one knee, taking my hand in one of his and holding his dagger in the other. He placed the hilt in my open palm. What was with the Aldar and their daggers?

"Let me be your defender, your ally, your comfort," Penn said. "Let me cherish what you cherish, need what you need, and love what you love."

I closed my hand around the dagger as I started to shake all over. I knew what was coming.

"Bel," Penn said. "May I be your husband?"

"Yes!" I barely had time to move the dagger aside before he stood and crushed me against him. I kissed him so hard I forgot where I was, who I was. I had noticed the difference in the words he said. He did not ask me to become his wife, as a human man would have, he asked for permission to be my husband.

"Well, this isn't what I expected to bring back from the market today," Alfez said as we separated. He and Idrigaina resolved to take us to Bargolan as soon as possible. "My cousin Tag is a man of influence and impatience. He will not hesitate to rally every soldier in Valley Glade and beyond to come after his daughter. We must go by carriage. Tomorrow."

"Out on the open roads? That's madness," Penn said. "Ships sail from this port to the continent—"

Alfez shook his head. "No ship's captain will take a human woman aboard without a marriage contract bearing the seal of the Sacred Order. It is a law that even the lowliest smuggler dares not break. So we go by land, in disguise. You and Idrigaina will pose as merchants, with Bel'eva and me as your *Mundin* servants."

As night fell, they made a bed of blankets for us on the floor of the sitting room, then retreated to their own attic bedroom. By now the effects of our soul bond had eased, but sleep did not come to me. Restless, I turned to watch Penn sleeping, all of him glowing warmly in the dying firelight from the nearby hearth. Unable to resist, I ran a finger along his jaw, then down to his chest. Both our brands had faded to invisibility since we left the fortress. Under my touch, Penn's flickered dimly. A touch made with pure intention. He stirred and opened his eyes.

"Are you afraid?" he asked.

"No," I said. "Just admiring my betrothed." For the first time, that title brought me joy instead of dread. I ruffled my hand through his hair. He groaned as I traced the pointed contour of his ear. Heat pulsed at my core. I dropped my hand beneath the blankets and found him ready for me as his lips found mine.

He lifted my leg over his side, bringing our hips together. He held himself against me, whispering in Aldarian as he rocked his body ever so slightly, until I was gasping and quivering with anticipation. Then he said, "I love you," and slid slowly into me.

I repeated the words back as my body clenched around the length of him. As passion built between us, both our soul brands began to glow. I covered his brand with my palm, pushing him down on his back and kneeling astride him. He gripped my hips and my hair. Tendons stood out taut on his neck as he watched me bring him into my core again and again.

This…for the rest of my life. A tavernkeeper's daughter and an Aldar prince. Two unlikely souls bound by love, by magic, and a good dose of foolishness. I wondered what stories the elders would tell about us. Most likely none. I almost laughed. "I suppose it's only fair for me to ask you," I said, breathless with the sensation of him. "May I be your wife?"

Penn didn't answer. I felt him tense beneath me, and his

pleasure became mine. After, as we lay in each other's arms, he pressed his lips to my cheek and said, "Yes."

I woke in the early dawn to a thunderous pounding. In the moments my mind took to drag itself free of sleep, I thought I was back at the fortress, its walls rattling around us as we repeated the incantation. Then my eyes settled on the comfortable furnishings of Alfez and Idrigaina's sitting room.

"What—" I started. Penn was crouched behind me, free of the blankets. When I started to speak, he put his hand over my mouth and dragged me protectively against his chest.

The pounding continued at the front door. "Alfez Hombord! Open in the name of the town guard."

"Alright, alright, I'm coming!" Alfez appeared from the stairs, sounding annoyed, but his eyes flashed to us warily. "Just give me a moment to dress. The sun's not even up, for saints' sake!"

Idrigaina slipped silently past him toward us, helping us dress and gather our things. She shoved the pile of blankets under the settee. Gesturing urgently, she brought us to the kitchen. With unlikely strength, she lifted a wooden table without a sound and pulled back the rug beneath it to reveal a trap door. She threw it open and the smell of cold, damp earth invaded the cozy scents of the cottage.

"This tunnel goes a quarter mile southwest," she whispered. "Once you are out, follow the creek east to where the trees are thickest, and you will find an old trail between curled oaks. It will take you south to the Harbors Road."

Penn laid a hand on her forearm and she flinched in surprise. "Come with us. They will kill you if they find out you helped us."

"Forgive me, your Highness, I cannot," she said, glancing at Alfez by the front door, still complaining loudly to distract the guards outside. "We may not be bound by ancient magic as you are, but my soul is his."

I knew she didn't mean it in the way I had been taught: that the husband was the keeper of all the souls in his household, guiding them away from sin and toward the virtues proclaimed by the saints. She meant that if their hearts should cease to beat, their love would not end.

Penn and I dropped down into the tunnel, and she closed the hatch over us. Penn whispered to reignite the fairy light in his lantern, casting the mud walls and wood beams in eerie blue. His words from a moment before echoed in my mind as we hurried downslope. Idrigaina would be killed for helping us. Probably Alfez too, after a long excruciating trial, broken up by terms locked in the public stocks. Their deaths would be my fault, as was Lus being whipped into a confession.

And if they caught us, a dark, damp place like this would become my home. The catacombs under the Sacred House, filled with the skulls of my ancestors, staring in judgement from black, empty-holed eyes.

Legs burning from running in a crouch, I stumbled. Penn didn't notice right away, leaving the darkness to surround me. He only turned when I moaned through my tears. All I could think of was the catacombs and gaunt women who inhabited them, the Unseen whose faces I'd only ever glimpsed for a few seconds as they dashed to do Lady Mordred's bidding.

Penn knelt in front of me, hand tight on my upper arm. "We must keep going."

"It's a tomb, it's a tomb," I muttered to myself, shaking my head.

"This is a smuggler's trail," Penn said, frowning. "Your cousin was wise to find a home with such an escape."

Penn seemed blessedly immune to panic, and it restored some of my sanity. "He didn't build this?"

"No," Penn traced a grubby finger along a rough beam. "These are timbers from the Pinebock woods, now gone for generations. This is an old route." He looked back at me. "Which means others may know of it. We must hurry."

After the longest quarter mile of my life, we emerged dirty and light-blind from beneath a rocky outcropping. We followed the creek and found the trees Idrigaina had described. The trail soon deposited us on the hardpack of the Harbors Road, which would guide us south to the coastal city of Bargolan.

Penn had cut all the trim from his stolen guardsman's uniform, turning the outfit into a nondescript wool suit. I reaffixed the matron veil atop my head, my hair coiled tight at the nape of my neck. Even cut short, far too much of Penn's bright hair showed for my liking, but there was no helping it. We could only hope any passersby took us for peasants.

We ran as much as we could, knowing that we were at a disadvantage on foot. Penn seemed like he could have run for half a day without stopping. I was surprised by how well I kept up with him. I had never had much stamina. Like most girls, I was discouraged from exertion. But the weakening effect that the soul bond had had upon us during our separation had the opposite effect now that we were together. My legs would not tire. As we hurried through the countryside, I began to have hope for our escape. Maybe foolish optimism was a side effect of the soul bond, too.

Hooves pounded on the dirt road behind us.

Logically, I knew who made up the King's forces from Valley Glade, but when they came upon us, I was surprised to see Nafene and Gabol Mordred at the head of the squad.

"Oh saints, no," I said. Penn grabbed me and we stepped to the side of the road with our heads down, submissive before the King's soldiers. All five of them spurred past us and I let out a breath of relief, then Gabol shouted and turned his horse. The three at the back of the pack notched arrows as Gabol and Nafene slid down from their saddles. Penn had no time to put me behind him as he had when Alfez approached us.

"Keep your eyes down," he said, but I knew it was too late.

"Remove your veil, sister," Gabol said, a hint of glee in his growling voice. He and Nafene came to a stop a few strides away.

"Brother," Penn said. "You dare not dishonor my wife with such a request."

I winced. Maybe it was because he was scared, or merely that he'd been speaking to Idrigaina in his mother tongue last night, but the barest hint of an accent clung to Penn's consonants. Through the fogginess of the veil, I saw Gabol's gaze switch to Penn. My heart thundered in the silence that followed.

Then Gabol yelled, "Aldar!"

I stepped forward, pushing Penn aside. An arrow meant for him tore through the soft flesh between my shoulder and neck, spinning me to the ground. I knew immediately that the wound was not bad. Penn did not, and he made a noise I hoped to never hear again, throwing himself over me, his back to the soldiers.

"I'm fine," I said, or thought I did, even as blood soaked the collar of my dress. "I'm fine. Just take off my veil. Do as he says."

"*Laehmiz catofaldet polusna eret,*" Penn said. He wasn't looking at me. His eyes were closed as he rose and turned, a dagger in each hand.

"Penn, no!"

"*Laehmiz catofaldet polusna eret,*" he said again. "*Faimae lex—*" Another arrow whistled toward him. In a flash of impossible speed, he knocked it aside with a blade, sending it to the ground behind us in a plume of dirt and leaves. With a wicked hiss of metal against leather, Gabol and Nafene drew their flared short swords.

"Do not speak your curses at us, demon," Nafene said. He raised his sword and started forward. Without a thought for my injury, I leapt to my feet and jumped in front of Penn so fast that one of his blades tore through my sleeve. My improvised matron veil lifted free of my hair and fluttered to the ground at my feet. Nafene halted with his sword tip an arm's length from my chest. The pain of my wound caught up with me a moment later and I tried not to vomit. I clutched my shoulder and stared at them.

"It *is* you," Nafene said.

"Step back!" Gabol roared at his cousin. He glanced over his shoulder at the mounted archers and raised a fist. They lowered their bows. Only now did I notice that one of them was Eget, Lus's husband. At least my friend would learn what had become of me. If he told her the truth, that is. "She is my betrothed," Gabol said.

"I am not," I said.

"By the laws of my people," Penn said. "She has granted me prior claim."

Rage shuddered Gabol's cheeks. "I don't care where you put your cock, ghoul. Whore or not, she was given to me!"

"Better his whore than your wife," I said.

Gabol lunged, and his growl blended with Penn's voice, "*Laehmiz catofaldet polusna eret, faimae lexka bannin.*"

Not thinking, I repeated his words as I had the incantation that revealed the soul bond. Eget and the other two archers dropped their bows and fell limp from their horses. I saw a glint of silver as Gabol stumbled. He landed on all fours, a claw clutching a crystal sphere protruding from his shoulder—the pommel of an Aldar dagger. Penn stepped forward and grabbed Gabol by the neck and spun him onto his back, holding the other dagger ready.

"Wait!" I shouted.

"Get the other!" Penn shouted back.

I turned to Nafene, who still had his sword pointed at me despite his wobbling knees. He swung as I lunged. The curse had had less effect on him than the others, but I was faster than his blade. I caught him above the knees with my full weight, diminished though it was in recent months. He tumbled back. I beat my fists on his forearm until he released the sword. I kicked it out of reach, then rammed my foot into his stomach until he curled up, blocking my blows.

"Bel." Penn said my name gently. He had his foot on Gabol's shoulder, opposite where the dagger was embedded. He held the other dagger toward me, hilt first, as he had when he asked if he could marry me. The question his eyes asked me now was very different.

I reached for the weapon. Gabol gasped, his eyes narrow with pain. I heard a shuffling behind me and turned, expecting to see Nafene crawling for his sword. Instead he was dragging himself through the dust toward us. His hand clasped his cousin's boot, and he started muttering. "Leave behind sin, carry only blessings. Leave behind cares, carry only grace. May his soul rest in the arms of the saints…"

It was a prayer. Nafene was giving Gabol his last rites. I looked at the dagger embedded in the soft flesh between Gabol's chest and his arm, then up at Penn.

"Is that a deadly wound?" I asked. "Do you know?"

"It might not be, if he does not shift the blade until he sees a healer."

I nodded, dropping my outstretched hand. Penn tucked the other dagger back into its sheath. "You wish to show mercy," he said.

Nafene sobbed and switched to a prayer of thanks.

"No," I said. "I think helplessness will be a much better punishment. Let them feel some small fraction of what I have felt."

We dragged the soldiers to the side of the road and tied them each to a tree. They stared at us with wide eyes, conscious despite their floppy, useless bodies.

"So you *can* utter curses," I said to Penn. I had come to believe that Aldar curses were another of the elders' lies. Being raised as I had, the truth should have scared me, but it didn't.

"I never said I could not. The one we said only works on those who truly believe themselves our enemy. Their hate for us was their undoing."

I looked at Gabol, holding myself still in his loathing gaze. I leaned over him, my face mere inches from his. He tried to rear away from me, but the sturdy tree trunk behind him would not let him. He was as powerless as I had been when he held me down and kissed me all those years ago. I spat into his pink-rimmed eyes.

"I have never been and never will be yours," I said.

We stripped Gabol and the others nearly bare. Luckily, one of the archers, Cadef, was nearly as tall as Penn, his uniform only slightly snug on the Aldar's larger form. Under the thick wool, my breasts would not be noticeable at a glance. I would pass for a soldier with my hair tucked into a cap. Penn took the bridles of two of the horses.

"Can you ride?" he asked.

Most human women did not, for fear it would spoil their childbearing anatomy in some way. "Not well," I admitted. "But I have seen it done often."

"I don't suppose it matters. We have to go," he said, and he helped me into the saddle. At first, I felt wobbly so high above the road. The pain of my shoulder wound—which Penn had bandaged with strips of a linen shirt—finally set in as I gripped the reins. My discomfort gave way to nerves as we continued south on the Harbors Road. Soon the sea appeared to our right, the expanse of blue whispering the promise of escape on its waves. But we were not able to flee yet.

Spires appeared on the misty horizon beyond the rolling hills, then the boxy forms of Bargolan's less lofty sprawl. The crowds on the city's streets parted before our horses, many heads nodding respectfully to our uniforms. Voice gruff with authority, Penn asked after the priest with the small chapel that Alfez and Idrigaina had told us about. The answers he got brought us to a quiet neighborhood in the shadow of the ancient university. The chapel was too humble for a spire, its façade adorned only by flowering vines curving around a small rosette window. In the quiet dimness inside, my breath grew shallow. I tried not to look at the saints staring down at us from the stained glass.

"How may I serve you, honored protectors?" A man with fine gray hair rose from his knees at the altar. Folding his hands in his robes, he strode calmly toward us. I studied him for some sign of his distant Aldar heritage, hoping to confirm he was the right man. I could not tell what color his hair had been in his youth. His cheekbones were hardly sharper than any other human's, his ears round. The only hint came from his bearing, a gliding walk that I'd noticed in Penn and others.

"Alfez and Idrigaina have sent us," I said. The priest halted at my woman's voice.

"Oh," he murmured, taking a closer look at me, then Penn. "I see. Please, follow me."

He led us out a side door, across a flower-speckled graveyard, to a one-story rectory. The inside was sparse but tasteful. Many of the few furnishings bore the elegant, tapered styling of Aldar carpentry, which Penn pointed out to me with wistful pride. The priest brought us to a study with tall windows facing southwest. Gauzy white drapes fluttered in the breeze off the sea.

"I'm Father Ughen," he said. "You say Alfez and Idrigaina sent you. I have a guess as to why."

I swallowed hard. Some deep, instinctual part of me still wanted to cower before the authority of the Sacred Order. I couldn't tell from Father Ughen's steady features what he thought of us.

"We need a marriage certificate in order to book passage on a ship," Penn said.

Father Ughen nodded. He studied us for another long moment. "I will not perform a false ritual."

"I have gold," Penn said. "And diamonds."

"This particular scruple of mine is beyond the reach of a bribe, my lord Aldar. Heretic though I may be, there are some elements of the sacred teachings that linger on from the time when our peoples' faiths were one. I am bound in my heart to follow them. I will only perform a ceremony if it proceeds from a place of honor."

"I have followed the traditions," Penn said. "I have come to her on my knees, presented my blades to her—"

"That's not what he means," I said, laying my hand on Penn's arm. "We love each other, Father. We wish to live our lives together."

"Very well," Father Ughen said. "You will be married."

I sighed with relief and took Penn's hand, leaning my head against his shoulder.

Father Ughen shook his head at Penn. "Bribery. You are thinking far too much like a human, your Highness. As one of your subjects—at least in part—I could hardly have denied a royal request, if you had made one. You might try that first, next time."

"In that case," Penn said. "May we have your drapes?"

The door flew open, sending said drapes flapping madly.

"Ughen!" Alfez burst into the room. Idrigaina shoved past him and pulled me and Penn into her long arms.

"Oh good," Father Ughen said in flat amusement. "Witnesses. Just in time."

"Heaven help me," Alfez gasped. "I saw the army horses outside and feared the worst."

"What happened with the town guards?" I asked as

Idrigaina released us.

"I have years of experience making them think I've given them what they want," Alfez said, "without giving them much at all."

"You would make a good silk merchant," Penn said.

"Speaking of which," Father Ughen said. "You said something about my drapes?"

In an hour, Penn and Idrigaina made me a dress from the gauzy white silk, to which they affixed the brocade bodice. When finished, it only vaguely resembled my Choosing gown. The skirts hovered above my toes, so walking was easy. The sleeves were long but split partway down my arm, allowing me free use of my hands. I had some scruples about having my shoulders exposed, not for any lingering religious modesty, but because of the bandage bound around my shoulder. Penn told me to wear my wound proudly.

"Does it befit an Aldar princess?" I asked, twirling for him.

"I do not think I'll be a prince anymore, so I cannot grant you the title," Penn said, then smiled. "But yes, it does."

We were married at sunset. Alfez walked me down the aisle, then joined Idrigaina in the front pew. In the Aldar tradition, Penn and I kneeled together in front of Father Ughen, instead of the bride bowing before the groom, as it would have been if I had married Gabol. We said our vows and he kissed me as the setting sun lit up the room, turning my dress to gold.

We signed the marriage certificate with new names that we gave each other. An hour later, in the harbor, we wrote them again in the ship's manifest. Our wedding night was spent in a berth so small that we could barely do our passions justice. Nevertheless, pressed heart-to-heart, our soul brands filled the cabin with a blue-green glow, sending shafts of light through the porthole, glittering on the night water of the port.

At dawn, the ship weighed anchor and filled its sails. Alfez and Idrigaina promised they would flee on another vessel, so when I gazed at the receding coast, there was very little my heart was leaving behind. All that I had given up had been replaced by my love for my red-haired Aldar, by our eternal bond, and the knowledge that whatever life lay ahead of me, it would be mine.

About the Author

DEVON LEE SOIFER lives with her husband in California in a cottage at the edge of the forest. She owns four lightsabers, at least a dozen wigs, and far too many books. When not writing, she's probably getting lost in a video game or a bookstore.